TIMOTHY R

Fated Knights

First edition

This book was professionally typeset on Reedsy.
Find out more at reedsy.com

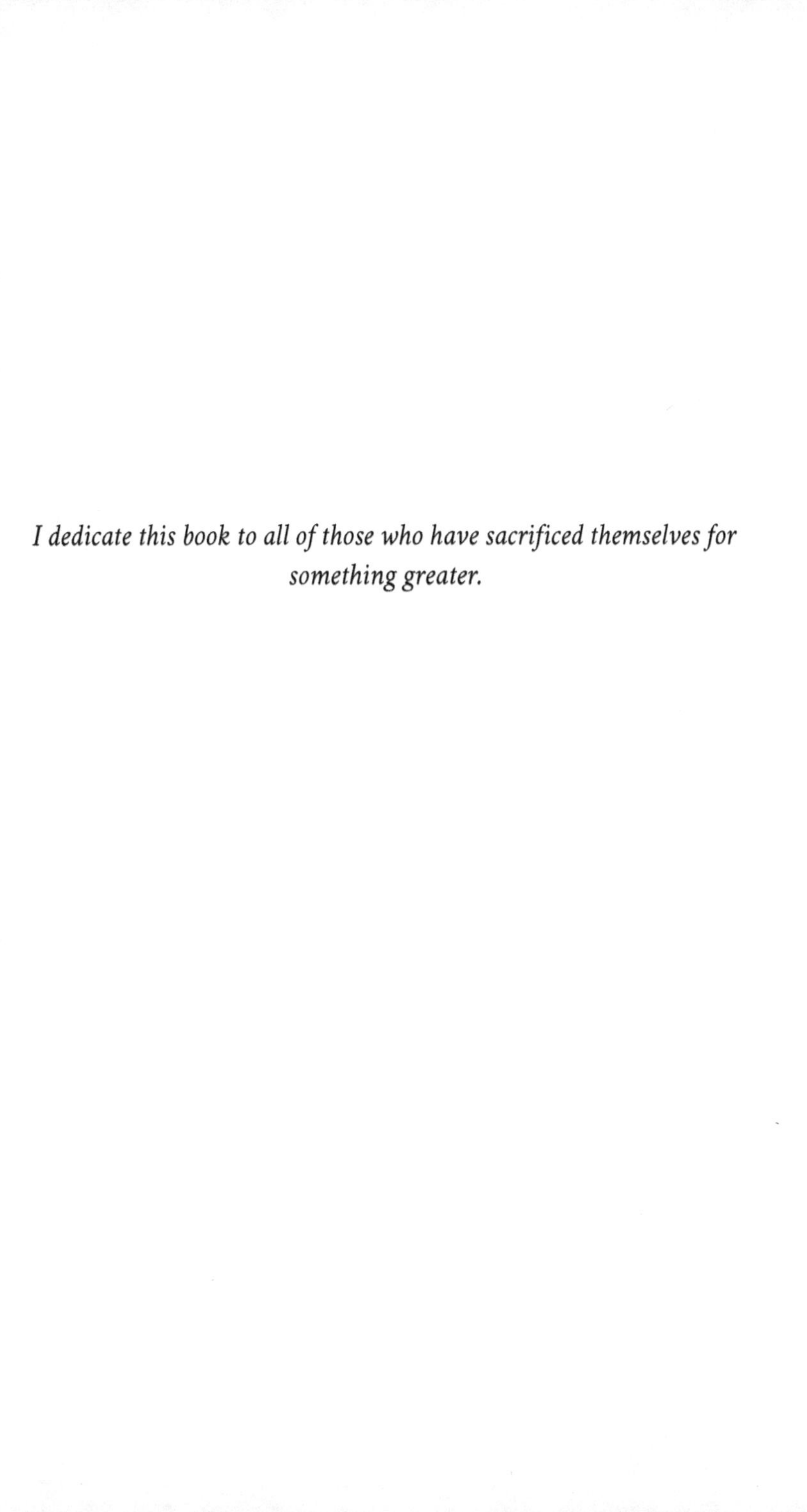

I dedicate this book to all of those who have sacrificed themselves for something greater.

Some are destined to die
some to shine as the sun,
many to turn to dust
threads of lives to come undone.
Only gods can live forever
I am but a man,
I fight for what I love
I die with sword in hand.
So give me love sweet mother
I am sorry I leave this world,
Be sure I slayed the other man
Know that I once loved a girl.
Heavens open wide
For a humble soldier comes to your
gate,
To the gods my hands are open
I hand to you my fate.

THE BALLAD OF THE GONE

Contents

Preface

This book was written as an inspiration from a post about leper knights that I once read. It is for adult audiences as there is cursing and intense action. As a fantasy author I took on this endeavor simply for the enjoyment of telling a fast paced story about some knights on the brink of death.

I hope you enjoy what I have created.

Acknowledgments

I'd like to acknowledge Brian Holshouser, Tora Brinn, Secret Stacy, along with others in the community for their support, especially in creation of this novella.

I'd also like to acknowledge Writers-journey services for their help with the cover.

Fated Knights

Timothy Robare

1

Chapter 1

I

Till Death Do Us Part

An assurance of death often wages against the hope of life, the desire for a miracle. Some succumb to it, while others wage war against it. It is almost as if the path to glory rests in the hands of death and fate. Hero, villain, or neither—it all ends the same.

Each step Alexander Riagani took upon the cobblestone path brought him one step closer to a place he wasn't meant to be. Purple cloth swaddled his face, revealing only his brown eyes above the wave of fabric. Similar cloth swallowed his hands so no skin showed. Slowing to a stop, he gazed at the gate to the home that used to be his. Grapevines crawled their way up the stone with their heart-shaped leaves and small bundles that were prepared to pick. Houses upon houses were built of the same brown stone as far as the eye could see.

The alley to the house was wider than some others that fell in on top of one another. Those who walked through the alley paid little attention to him. Heat beat upon the stone from the sun above. It took Alexander longer to reach the city than he thought it would, but maybe it was his fault. Excited terror swelled inside of him like a raging fire.

Under Alexander's wrapped face, sweat began to cover his olive skin. Inhaling, his chest swelled, and he attempted to step through the gate. He seemed to be a tree; the step was much more difficult to take than he realized. Another breath. Another. There was no choice, it was time. The small gate opened up to a small courtyard with five stairs leading to the house. Alexander gazed upon a home he had not set eyes upon in three years—since he was banished to the city of Assin, the colony of death.

Water flowed into the plants from the watering can gripped by the delicate hands of his wife, Entienne. She was surrounded by orange, clay pots of various sizes with trees and vegetables that sprouted from them in luscious greens. The woman had not lost a beat; it was as if she hadn't aged a day. Wavy black hair flowed to her mid back like waves from the sea. Slender body with a curve of the hips that led to a butt that made any man take a second look. Those calves, he bit his lip, calves that a goddess would murder for even out of jealousy. How many fights had he got in because of that ass alone? As if she could feel someone watching, she looked behind her and jumped with her hand to her chest.

"What do you want?" the beautiful woman could have a tone like a viper. "Ballsy beggar to enter someone's home."

"It's me, Entienne."

She dropped her watering can, eyes growing wide as two moons. Water ran through the cracks of the dry stone, cascading down the stairs.

"What are you doing here, Alexander? If the city guards catch you, you'll be hanged like a common thief."

"I have been dead for quite a long time now, wife. There is a heart beating inside of me, but nothing else. I had to lay eyes upon you one last time. As radiant as the sun ever was. As gorgeous as any moon. It is as if you haven't aged a day since we last saw each other. The image of you never leaves my thoughts. I remember the last kiss we had before…before I caught this."

Alexander glanced at his covered hands, disgusted at the thought of the wounds that festered underneath. Looking at the house, it was difficult to recall the day soldiers came to drag him from the home his family built. From Alexander's young son and his beautiful wife. It was difficult to know when he caught the sickness, it almost seemed as if the gods picked at random.

"So long ago, those lips seemed everything worth fighting for and that remains true today. Now my heart beats true again, just at the sight."

"Alex…" Her mouth twitched but she stood frozen.

"It is okay, Entienne. You do not need to say what I already know. I just wanted to see you and our son one last time." He raised his hand as if to touch her but knew he couldn't. It would mean sending her to a miserable death as well. Desire conquered by justice, but turmoil boiled inside of him. A monsoon of anger prepared to be unleashed upon the world. "Soon I may die. It has been years, but you linger. In my dreams I can touch your face, your back, everywhere. I can feel you, then I wake alone to the ghost of you. Our son, I know he has grown much since I have been gone. I imagine he is a strong boy."

"Seeing you will be too difficult for him. He is at school anyways."

Alexander's head sank and his chest ached with a burning pain that caused his knees to wobble. It took all he had to not fall to his knees.

"Can you let him know I died a hero?" he looked up at her again.

"What do you mean? What are you talking about Alex?" Entienne stepped forward but then took a quick step back as she fumbled with her hands.

"I have a plan. A plan that will mark me as a hero or a fool. I am going to battle the Higani. If I am to die, it will be with a sword in my hand fighting for our gods and battling for you and our son. I will no longer rot in Assin. I will die doing something honorable. Something worthy of the time I have left. The Higani, they are monsters that wish to force their god upon us. They want everyone to believe in their one true god, their savior. For too long they have plagued the lands, swallowing them like shadows. I must stand for something, if I cannot hold you, then at least I can hold a sword."

"Alex…" Entienne grabbed her dress and crinkled it in her hands.

"I love you. I have always loved you. You were always the brightest star on the darkest night. You have always been my strength. Loving you is the greatest thing I have ever done and nothing else will come close. Without your touch I'm half a man. Without your love, I feel more dead than this disease causes. I can't watch our son grow. I can't love you; I can't touch you. The least I can do is something worthwhile." He held her gaze that told him her heart still beat for him.

"I have always loved you, Alex. I will always love you. That will never change." A tear streamed from her face and she leaned against the brown stone house.

Entienne was a strong woman, but there was pain in her face as those doe eyes stared into his.

"But it can never be," he interrupted her. "I want you to find love again. I want you to have a good life. I will keep you in my heart." His closed fist moved onto his chest. "For you, I will slay men who threaten our way of life. It is all I have left. I will cut them down until I no longer can. It will all be in your name, Entienne. My love for you will wreak havoc upon the field of battle when the rage that is built up within me will finally be unleashed." Turning away, Alexander hesitated.

"Alex," she said.

He paused, his hand pressing against the brown stone of the gate that led to the street.

"We love you. I hope you find what you are searching for. You are a good man; you don't need redemption. You have always been honorable. You have always been kind." Trembling, she couldn't take it anymore and fell to her knees, weeping with her head in hands.

"All men need redemption." Those would be his last words to her.

It was impossible to stay any longer. If he did then he would have to grab her and feel her like they used to. Firm in his hands, gasps and shrieks, they seemed like yesterday's memories but were mere remnants of a life so long ago. It seemed impossible not to fall to his knees with her, hold her, comfort her, but Alexander could not send his wife to her doom.

Alexander waited until he rounded the corner to lean against the wall and allow the tears to rupture from his face, battling against the dry air. For so long, Alexander felt dead and defeated. He still remembered the moment he was forced from his home. Five men he had rendered unconscious. Five more men filled their spots and he took a beating with no other choice. His young son and Entienne crying as he fought and got beat down until finally there was nothing left to do. Now tears gushed as if his face turned into a fountain. The cloth around his nose and mouth dampened, giving him a small respite from the heat above. Sliding down the warm wall, his face fell into his knees. None of the passerby's acknowledged his existence. He was alone.

2

II

Assin

Assin was a long trek back. Only one dirt road meant for necessities to be delivered. Each step plagued Alexander with the thoughts he would never see home again. A concept he knew from when he was banished, but now it was confirmed. Joints felt swollen and parts of his skin under his clothes were shedding from the mixture of itchiness and pain. His large black horse drank from a pond next to a tree she was tied to. A well-trained companion was difficult to come by, but she never strayed far.

"Hey, Canyon." Alexander ran his hand upon her chin while she whinnied.

Alexander leaned his forehead against the white stripe on the horse's that ran down between her eyes.

"Let's go girl." He tightened the girth and climbed on. "We have quite the journey ahead of us."

Many trees filled along the sides of the road to give shade for the journey and made him feel less alone on the desolate path. Once a month deliveries were made to the disease-ridden city, other than that, the road was unused. A path to death—to those without the sickness. Dust billowed into the sky as hooves struck earth with a steady drum. Ahead, a black stone arched over the path—sleek, black obsidian to signify the beginning of Assin, a symbol of death. Sleek, black obsidian. Small houses popped up a distance from the path, until they became tighter the closer to the small city he moved. Alexander moved with the rhythmic trot of the black mare. Arriving home, he watched his brother hard at work under the afternoon sun. Getting down from his horse, Alexander gave her a pat, then walked toward him.

"Brother, where did you go?" Chase looked up from the wood he chopped.

The log splintered with a crack as drops of sweat rolled down the muscular chest and shredded back of tanned skin. Flesh was dotted with black sores that made him appear part leopard.

Chase was several years younger than Alexander, and still wore his hair in the longer style, tied back to keep out of his eyes. Both brothers had gone to war together years prior. That was before they caught the disease that now plagued them. Alexander moved to hug his brother who's sweat caused him to feel more like a frog than a man. Hugs were important for those who were shunned from society, unable to be touched by most.

"I needed to get out. I made a decision last night."

"Hmm?" Chase eyed him with his still youthful curiosity as his axe ripped through another piece of wood.

"We will go to war. I am thirty-four. Sounds like a good age to die. I always liked that number."

"War? With whom?" Chase stared at his brother with eyebrows furrowed.

"We will go fight the Higani. Who else would we fight? Has the disease rattled your brain?"

"I am splitting wood and you come home speaking of war, how would I know? You actually think they will let us leave?" Chase laughed. "Perhaps, the disease has grabbed hold on your brain." His index finger pressed against the side of Alexander's skull. "We are trapped here. This is our burial ground."

"The guards have all left. I've been taking trips around the perimeter for months and haven't seen a single one."

"How long have you been planning this?" Chase stared, his lips tightened.

"Quite some time, brother. I need something to live for as I stare down death on a daily basis. Don't tell me you are ecstatic about staying in this city of the dying. Every day new diseased come, and every day others die. This trivial life where everything we loved is behind us. We can ride off to war and make a difference in our final moments. We can protect those we love and die in a worthwhile manner, not sitting here, digging in the earth until we become a part of it."

Chase grumbled a plethora of words that Alexander couldn't hear but hoped his brother would follow him regardless.

"Care to speak up? Can't hear you."

"Two men to go to war?"

"No." Alexander laughed as his hand collapsed upon Chase's shoulder. "I have much more than that in mind. An army."

"I don't know if I love the sound of that. We have to go to church soon. You should change. An army? Will we just raise it out of the ground? Did you gain magic I don't know of?"

"I will go like this and perhaps. You call it magic; I call it hope.

I will raise an army. Follow and see."

"Like…" Chase gulped. "That? You look like you were on trail for a week. You are supposed to go to church clean, Alex."

"Good. Let's call it a statement. None of us are *clean.* Not in the eyes of everyone else. We are forsaken, filthy, and shunned."

Shaking his head Chase went and changed, while Alexander tended to Canyon. The brush cruised through dense black fur of the warhorse.

"At least I don't need to convince you to come with me. A trusty steed to the end," he laughed to himself. "I am glad to have you at my side and under my sore rear."

The large head nuzzled Alexander, ruffling his already disheveled hair.

"Ouch." A piece of gray skin broke away from his hand, letting loose a small flow of blood. "Fucking disease." Alexander rubbed the dense, flaking skin then looked up to see his brother making his way toward him. "Finally, let's go praise the gods."

"Mhmm. I hope the gods don't strike you down the moment we get there due to your lack of cleanliness. Looking like you crawled from the depths of the underworld."

"Worse things have happened. Brother." Both hands slapped onto Chase's face. "We are on the cusp of greatness. For ages we will be remembered, for instead of rotting, we picked up our swords and went to war."

Chase narrowed his eyes. "There might be something very wrong with you aside from Bentillux."

"The only thing wrong with me besides Bentillux is hope and faith."

The brothers joined in the line of sick as they flooded toward the church. Thin cloth draped from some that covered every inch of their body to defend against the sun. The building stretched up to a bell tower with a small golden dome. A loud toll announced the coming sermon.

"Let me help you." Alexander put a grey-haired man's arm around his shoulder. "Your leg, Mr. Gend, is it worse?"

A grimace took over the old man's face as he raised his baggy, tattered grey pant leg to reveal a festering wound of purple and black that threatened to swallow his shin.

"It is my time soon," Mr. Gend attempted to sound positive. "Finally, I will get to lay at rest."

"Don't talk like that."

"My wife succumbed to the disease before I was shipped here, Alexander. I am prepared to meet her again. I only wish I did more before now. Now I can never do anything else aside from limp across the land until the day my dear, Ellenda greets me. Can't say I know exactly which side she is on, but gods be good."

What can I say to a man who is facing what I will soon enough— festering wounds, body destroying itself, and there is nothing left to do aside from wait to die.

They passed through the oak doors, carved with winged creatures that stretched to a shining sun, everyone began to take their seats. Candles flickered along the walls up to a podium where the revered, Timothy Gallux stood with a smile that threatened to swallow his face whole. Behind him stood three smaller statues to portray each of the three gods, watching over all of those before them.

"You'd never know he was one of the dying the way he smiles," Chase whispered, his eyes glaring at the man behind the podium.

"That is part of faith, brother. When a man has nothing left, he can at least cling to hope."

"Mhmm." Chase rolled his eyes.

"We are in church. Don't tell me you have lost faith."

"I question it at times."

Timothy was among the youngest in Assin at twenty-five. His ruddy, clean-shaven face gave him the appearance of a teenager.

"Welcome, brothers, sisters. Thank you for joining me. I am glad to be here today." He opened a thick book with faded red and navy-blue binding. With a vast smile he looked over the crowd. "I will start with a quick reading from the Book of Nasir. 'Listen, all who come. Yenna, the mother of all, goddess of war and love, speaks to thee. There is a time for war and a time for love. Love is war within itself. Love thy neighbor, love thy friend, and love thy family. Love thy enemy enough to show them compassion, even with a dagger at their throat.'

"Perfect quote." Alexander stood up and all eyes turned to him.

"What are you doing, you idiot?" Chase tugged at his sleeve. "Sit down. For the love of the gods."

Shaking off his brother's hand, Alexander strolled down the aisle, head held high. Eyes watched him like a thousand hawks.

"Brother, Alexander. What can I do for you?" Timothy reached out his arms with white fabric that draped loosely.

Covered in fine, white robes with a purple chasuble with golden crescent moons that draped over them, the younger man was an image of purity.

"Priest Timothy has stated an important message. I have a feeling from Yenna," Alexander announced.

Gasps filled the full church. Chase sank his head to hide, attempting to vanish behind the oaken pew, hand over his face so no one could recognize him.

Alexander looked everyone over and then began. "We are all dying. There is no question. We have been sentenced to death by both disease and our countrymen." He stared at the holy book near him, then back to the crowd. "A city has been built for us and by us. We survive, sure. We are surviving in isolation together until the disease strikes us from this land. The headsman awaits us, blade sharpened. There is a better fate. A way to make a difference in this world before we leave it." Alexander paused and attempted to make eye contact with each person in the crowd. "There is nothing more dangerous than a man who desires death."

"What are you talking about, Alexander?" Timothy's smile faded into puzzlement.

"We can go to war. We will be our own army to redeem our land against the Higani." His fist pounded against his heart. "Many of us left loved ones behind, children, wives, grandchildren, husbands, and so much more. This disease has taken so much from us. Under Yenna's guidance, we can march and take battle to the enemy. If we die, let us die doing something good, not withering like dried grapes. Let us sharpen our blades and seek glory! Think of all that has been stolen from us. All they threaten. When we are gone, they may very well consume all of the lands and force everyone into their ways of life." He took a step toward the crowd. "Do you want to die here, in isolation, or do you want to stand, sword in hand, and vanquish the an enemy one last time?"

"You speak blasphemy!" an older woman yelled. "You wish to send our husbands and sons off to war."

Shouts erupted like a geyser with so much noise that it was impossible to comprehend what anyone was saying. Alexander watched with a smile while everyone vomited anything that came to mind. Timothy's head shook side-to-side with slow motions.

"People. People." Timothy let out a sigh. "Silence!" he shouted. "Praise the gods." The younger man adjusted his robes with a firm grip.

Alexander let out a surprised laugh, impressed at the younger man's ability to exert authority.

"I think Brother Alexander has a valid idea." Timothy gave a small nod.

"You do?" Chase's head perked up.

"I do. Yenna is the goddess of war. Why would she not want such a thing? All of us are condemned to death. Why should one not pick up the sword in the name of our gods? We have been sentenced to stay here, that is true, but on our own, why not shelve our burden and die for our gods?"

Another eruption of gasps and murmurs discharged in the church. Sun filtered through intricate stained-glass windows of blue, red, orange, and green. Alexander looked at Timothy and gave a nod of approval which Timothy returned.

"If any wish to follow Alexander, you have my approval."

"Will you follow?" Alexander asked.

The priest was caught off guard, but his smile did not fade. He cleared his throat. "In days of darkness, we hold tight to life while walking the lines of death. Oh, sweet raven above, with eyes in the sky. You wander the world and see it all, watching both life and death." All eyes watched Timothy wondering what he would say. "I will."

Silence consumed the room. Not so much as a breath escaped a mouth.

Timothy sighed. "My skin festers. My heart weakens. I am younger than many here, that is true. Perhaps this is the great calling." He paced back and forth as every pair of eyes trailed his movement. "This could be the meaning of this vile disease.

II

The great calling that there is nothing left, but a glorious death in the name of our gods. Light versus darkness. A meaning behind why our skin bursts with sores, why our bones feel as if they have been grinded like olives to make oil, or why we have been sent away from the world we loved. This is the moment where we decide what fate we wish to hold; I will hold a sword and give my fate to the gods."

Silence shattered as each person discussed their options and began to shout in all directions. Alexander grabbed Timothy's shoulder.

"I am glad to have you at my side," Alexander said.

Timothy nodded. "It will be good to hold a sword again. The only place I ever truly found peace was in the moment of steel against steel where death was inevitable for one or the other. That is where the gods roam."

"A bit poetic, but I like it. I should go see Val Ron." A smirk crossed Alexander's face.

"I shall calm the heated minds of these people." Timothy eyed the crowd consumed by whispers.

As Alexander walked through the church, some eyes looked on with hope, while others glared with contempt. Chase leapt up, following his brother.

"Where to now?"

"Val Ron. We need armor if we are to go to war."

"We have armor though."

"We need armor to look similar. We will look the part. If we are to die, let us die with grace and beauty."

"What if our own view of us as an enemy?" Chase asked. "I am not sure as many shared your sentiment as you think."

"One thing at a time, brother." Alexander put a hand on each of his brother's shoulders. "All will be well. They will come, you will see. I believe."

"Armor upon achy bones and a long journey sounds like a recipe for doom."

Chase disagreed with Alexander but followed him regardless. A good younger brother. Chase had always been behind Alexander for every great moment, even when they disagreed, they would never turn their back on the other. Through the city streets they weaved. The wide sandstone made Assin easy to navigate. Hammer on steel echoed as they grew closer to the heat of the blacksmith's shop. Sweat swelled upon their foreheads the moment they entered.

"Val Ron." Alexander moved to greet the wide man.

"Gods be damned. To what do I owe this displeasure?" cheeks bounced as the large man laughed.

Large eyes gazed over a wide, hooked nose. Val Ron stood, his broad shoulders and barrel chest covered by a dark, leather apron. A hard man, once one of the most famous blacksmiths in the entire land.

"Armor." Alexander grabbed the blacksmith's forearm, firm as steel.

"Ha. For what? Are we going to war?" returned the gesture with a curious look.

"Yes." Alexander smiled.

Hard, brown eyes glared at him for a moment until Alexander didn't say anything else. Then a grunt stemmed from the massive chest.

"I want in. Bring me steel. Any you can find. Each person needs to come and get fitted, aye?"

"I will bring you steel and I will bring you people."

"This will be a good final endeavor. My bones and skin can't take much more. Each day it grows more difficult. More painful.

The heat breaks as much as it helps." Val Ron studied his hands the size of anvils with cracked, grey skin. One crack oozed with puss that caused the large man to grimace. "I will scrap what I can as well. It will be the best project I have ever done and my last I think."

"Honored to be at your side once more, my friend." Alexander slapped the other man's bulging back.

"It has been quite some time since we stood on a battlefield together. I remember mending your armor all too often. I will have to make it extra dense."

"Good, it can match his skull," Chase interrupted. "I doubt any sword can pierce that dense dome."

A laugh stemmed from the blacksmith that all but shook the ground underneath them.

"You aren't wrong about that," Val Ron agreed.

"I owe you my life. Not that I have much left of it."

"You owe me nothing."

"Now what?" Chase asked.

"Oh, follow me. Much more to do." Alexander slapped his brother's back.

3

III

Drunken Disease

Alexander shoved a handful of flatbread into his mouth. Water poured from a curved glass into his mouth, causing the bread to turn to mush. His brother gazed at him with furrowed brows.

"Let's go." Alexander's cheeks puffed out like a chipmunk.

"Where now?"

"You'll see."

With the sun below the horizon, the temperature grew more relaxed. The brothers made their way back toward the center of town. Hookers in thin pieces of cloth that strained to cover any piece of their body called out for customers. Flesh of sores mattered not to those whose souls danced within the fire. Screeches of fighting cats and drunken fights filled the next alley.

"Are we just out for a nightly jaunt in the worst part of the city?" Chase inquired.

"So many questions... Just come. When did you question every single step of life?" Alexander grabbed his brother's arm and tugged him along.

Through a dingy side door, murky shadows drifted among the dim lit room draped in silence.

"You wanted to get a drink and chose The Mule? Seriously?" Chase sighed. "There are much better taverns than this shithole. Coming here is asking to be punched in the face or stabbed." He eyed the characters in the room, the hardest of men and women in Assin. Some that the people of the world were happy to get rid of. One man with half a hand from some battle or another with a face that looked as if it was stitched together with the sheer amount of scars.

Alexander's middle finger snapped against his brother's nose.

"Did you just flick me?" Chase slapped his hand. "What in the gods has gotten into you?"

"Grab some ale. I see the target." Alexander dropped five coppers into his brother's hand.

"Target," Chase muttered as he moved toward the grim bartender. The man was tall and intimidating and he only had one eye, which he kept covered with a tiny black eye-patch with a skull on it.

On the opposite end of the bar sat a man facing the wall. He wore a dark, ruffled tunic, and his black hair fell across the fabric in thick waves.

"Adrian Tallamay, my old comrade." Alexander took a wide sweep around him to the opposite side of the booth. The table was covered in a multitude of obscenities carved by various blades.

Ale dripped from the coarse beard streaked in white, but the man didn't look up from the clay mug. Eyes gazed down into the liquid as if it were a magical potion.

"Do you intend on drowning yourself in ale until you die?" Alexander leaned forward.

Still, the man ignored Alexander and continued to drink.

"Don't you want to go out with glory at your fingertips? Reaching in and grabbing death by the balls and severing them with a blade? There is one thing you have always been good at and that is killing."

Being in charge of so many, Alexander knew those with the talent of killing. Few he had ever seen were better than the bulky man in front of him. Adrian was a vicious warrior that Alexander had seen deal death like few others.

Dark eyes tilted up at him.

"Ah, got your attention." Alexander gazed into two liquid pools of obsidian. "Good."

"We came for Adrian?" Chase wandered over with two mugs of frothy ale. "I will sit over here. If you beat him, it wasn't my choice to come." Setting one mug down in front of his brother, Chase sat across the slender space in a separate booth from the other two.

"I am building an army to go and fight the enemy. Those of us who are dying have nothing to live for anymore." Alexander leaned back and took a large swig from the mug. We drift along this void, pretending as if we are still going on with our lives, but we aren't. We do nothing but pretend." He leaned in to match the man's gaze. "Let's face death with sword in hand. I have seen you. I know you. None are better with a sword than you are, Adrian."

"Well, maybe Timothy," Chase interrupted.

"Let me die in peace," Adrian grumbled.

"Die in glory." Alexander's fist slammed against the table.

Adrian ignored the outburst and circled back to the prior point. "That cunt is not better than me with a sword. Go, now."

Alexander's hand reached over, grabbing the thick head of hair, and slamming Adrian's face against the table. Chase stood on the booth seat with wide eyes. Ale flew in all directions as the two clashed on their feet; Alexander received a hefty hook that reddened his cheek. In a melee of blows, the two bounced off tables and walls. Blood poured like a stream onto Adrian's beard, covering the white streaks. Then he grinned with red stained teeth and began to laugh. Two more punches opened a small gash on Alexander's cheek. Touching the blood on his face, Alexander laughed, then landed a punch into the other man's gut that was followed by an uppercut. Then Adrian laughed again.

Everyone around them sat back down in silence as both of the bloody faced men continued to cackle.

"Let's go to war then. Chase, you chicken livered cock sucker." Adrian shoved him over. "Standing on a booth like a coward. I would have knocked both of your heads together."

"I don't want my head knocked," Chase replied. "I actually prefer *not* being pummeled."

"You smell terrible." Alexander sniffed Adrian from afar.

With a tilt of his head, Adrian lifted his shirt to his broad nose, and chuckled. Then he shrugged it off.

"How are you?" Alexander adjusted his shirt and wiped blood from his nose.

"Drunk, mate. Very drunk. But feeling good! Even with this disease I can kill five hundred of those scum to the east. How big of an army do we have? I want to rip off their cocks and shove them up their own asses." Adrian guzzled some ale and a belch erupted from the behemoth of a man.

"Vile." Chase shook his head.

"Four of us at the moment. Others will join though. When is the last time you washed that grease pot you call hair?" Alexander laughed. "You might be able to cause them to surrender just at the sight and smell of you."

"Do you come here to get me to take a bath, mate? Keep insulting me and I will crush your head and fill my mug with your blood."

Before Alexander could answer he received a punch to the abdomen that sent air exploding from his chest. He bent over the table, gasping. Alexander took a deep breath to regain composure while Adrian continued to drink.

"No more questions. Let's hear this plan of yours."

"Blood and glory my friend, blood and glory." Alexander stood and slapped him on the back as he regained his breath.

Wading through the haze of smoke from pipes, they made their way out to the streets back toward Alexander and Chase's home. In great depth the trio spoke around a fire as ashes fluttered to the star filled sky. Bottle pressed to his lips; Adrian constantly took large swigs. If ale fish existed, the man was one. Moonlight lit white robes that drifted toward them like a ghost in the night.

"Is that a ghost or is this ale twisted?" Adrian eyed the liquid inside the bottle. "Sometimes I see ghosts, but not like this."

Alexander's hand drifted toward his pommel. His fingers danced upon the metal, his mind preparing itself for what was to come.

"Timothy?" Chase squinted.

"Good eyes, brother Chase." Timothy gave a faint chuckle.

"You had me thinking I saw a ghost." Adrian spit.

"Charming. May I?" Timothy gestured to a log.

"By all means. What brings you out here?" Alexander released the hilt of his sword.

"I believe you know. Unless today in church was a figment of my imagination." Timothy rubbed his sword hands together near the fire. "Your words sparked the faith inside of me. I stand and give sermons, I pray for those that are dying, but I am more of a statue than anything else. Wielding a blade again in the name of our gods, our faith, that would be a true testament. I love the church, but I wish for more. I wish to bathe the land in the blood of our enemies. Like Ezara Olax and Benkar Iglees, warriors of Yenna who fought against the ancient Kellarians."

"Woah." Adrian held up the bottle toward the warrior priest.

A dismissal with a wave of his hand with a cold gaze.

Timothy dismissed the offer with a wave of his hand and a cold gaze. "No alcohol will touch these lips. Poison may drift through my veins, but I will not swallow it from a sin filled bottle."

"More for me." Adrian shrugged.

"After you left, the church was divided. I believe about four hundred will follow us."

"Four-hundred-four. I like that number. Almost sounds divine." Alexander smirked. "I was working on something. I am no artist but wanted a symbol. I drew this symbol." Pulling out a piece of parchment, he revealed a drawing of snake.

"Why a snake?" Timothy eyed it.

"We will be the snakes in the weeds. They will not see us coming, but when they do, we shall strike with deadly intent. Bites that kill with no regard."

"Vicious. I accept it." A broad smile swept across Adrian's bearded face. "If I am to die, I will rip down the enemy throat by throat."

"This is why we are glad to have you on our side," Alexander laughed. "We will be brothers to the death. Let the gods shine their favor upon us as we honor them with the blood of the enemy."

"Lord Timothy, coming to join us? Maybe the gods do have some hope for us after all." Chase added.

"Once upon a time a lord. All titles stripped. No money aside from what my family gave me upon leaving. Just the same as you all. A sick man, in a sick city, destined to die." Timothy glared into the fire. The flame lit up his blue eyes. "I am prepared to die. I want to show the gods what I am made of. At times I feel as if they have forsaken me no matter how much I honor them. No matter how much I pray or how much I try to help others. Regardless, I have been handed a disease that I can't heal from. Even with all of this, I honor them. I will not turn my back even though it feels they have on us. I am only a man. Who am I to question the gods?"

Three pairs of eyes watched him but hardly seemed to breathe.

"That is why I drink," Adrian cut through the veil of silence.

The night was spent sharing stories of their pasts. Aside from Adrian who became belligerent and attempted to wrestle everyone. No matter how often Timothy declined the proposition, Adrian pestered him.

"Have you become a man yet? Any hairs on those little balls of yours?" Adrian attempted to grab between Timothy's legs.

"What is wrong with you?" Hand slapped against hand with immense speed.

"I hope we are doing the right thing," Chase said.

"The gods will let us know."

After having enough, Timothy left and Adrian passed out.

III

The two brothers moved inside.

4

IV

Waking Up to Wander

Waking up later the next morning, Chase found his brother loading armor into a sun-bleached, white oak cart.

"Too much noise," Adrian groaned. "So loud. It must barely be daylight."

"It has been day for hours yet," Alexander laughed. "Whatever metals you have, I need them."

Words muttered from under the thick beard as Adrian pushed himself off the ground with a grunt. Within the hour he returned, dragging a surprising amount of armor.

"Not my sword though. That remains."

"Of course."

At the town gate, Timothy awaited with three carts of armor, each pulled by enormously fat donkeys.

"As you requested. All that wish to come have given what they have. I hope you know what you are doing."

"I don't. I am leaving that to the gods." Alexander slapped the other man's shoulder and smiled. "Don't be so glum, Timothy. There is sun above, armor to be shaped, and swords to be swung. I hope you aren't out of practice."

"I am never out of practice. I was trained by Gregor Tallianus. One of the greatest swordsmen to exist. I practice every morning and every night with the moon. I could slice through the three of you like cheese left in the sun."

"I was trained by the enemy trying to take my head. None succeeded. I must be pretty great." Adrian pushed through the pair.

"Lovely." Timothy dusted at his clean lavender colored tunic. "I am so glad that you found that mongrel in whatever bottle he was hiding in."

"That mongrel might save your life."

"There is no one who can save my life." Timothy grimaced.

"Come, come. None of that. Let's go. We run on optimism and faith."

Through the town they weaved with silent eyes that stalked their steps. People danced to the side to avoid them, while others slapped their backs with joy. Once they made it to the blacksmith, they piled the armor high in front of him like a small mountain.

"Gods be good, that is a lot." Thick fingers scratched Val Ron's head as he eyed it. "I will melt it down, but I need measurements. Each person must come and have the armor fitted—that way you look like a proper unit."

"Of course. Also, here is this." Pulling out the parchment, Alexander handed it to the blacksmith.

Fingers like sausages grabbed the parchment, with eyes narrowed, Val Ron peered at the work and made small grunts.

"You want this upon the chest then?"

"Can you do it?"

Erupting with a guffaw, the blacksmith clutched his chest, leaving the other three to stare at one another in confusion.

"I could do it if I was blind and piss drunk. I will make your armor. I have found enough material for cloaks. It is this color. The only one I have found enough of." Reaching behind him he pulled out admiral-blue linen.

"That is perfect. There is enough for four-hundred-four of us?" Alexander rubbed the material.

Large lips pinched together as the blacksmith stared at Alexander.

"Gods be good. I hope Yenna appreciates this and takes my soul into her favor. Otherwise, you better slay every last one of those bastards."

"I will take that as a yes."

"Let me get your measurements. You will be the first four done. Come. Let's go," he rushed them. "I have a lot to do."

It took three weeks of constant work while the city swelled with intense emotions. A mixture of excitement and pride against hesitation and fear. Like two storms rushing against one another, but still the four moved.

"Today is the day." Alexander smiled at the line of the four-hundred prepared to receive their armor.

A small breeze drifted through the early morning, bringing the scent of adventure and fear.

"I did something special for you four." The blacksmith revealed their silver armor.

From bottom to top protruded a snake that with a quick look, appeared real. Golden shoulder pauldrons with the wide head of a snake clung to each set with small red stones for their eyes, glimmering from the sun's rays.

"The pauldrons are to set you four apart. The heads of the snake I suppose." The man chuckled. "Any venom that strikes will be from your mouths."

"They are spectacular. You have outdone yourself." Alexander studied each feature of the broad, spade-shaped head with a forked tongue that showed. Small indents created the effect of scales. "I am impressed and thankful."

"Blessed be Yenna."

"Blessed be Yenna."

One after the other, men of all ages stepped forward to receive their armor with the stunning, admiral blue cloaks. Singular pieced chest plates with separate forearm greaves. Below were long iron skirts in three pieces to allow for movement that stopped above the knees. Greaves of the shin also had small snakes that stretched from bottom toward the top.

"Now we are an army! Yenna will march with us toward the enemy! She will guide our feet and our swords. I have no intention of returning to Sinna. I have no intention to return anywhere. We will welcome death as much as we bring death upon the enemy. None of us will make it back home. All of us will die on the battlefield and be welcomed to the heavens to dine with the gods!"

Rectangular shields clanged as fists, daggers, and swords hit against them. For three weeks they had all trained non-stop. For three weeks they had waited for the moment when the true journey would begin.

"I am with you, brother." Chase watched over the crowd.

"I never had a doubt."

5

V

The Road from Death to Death

Assin was close to the border of the peace lands which worked out in their favor. Three days of marching brought them to the mighty Grandik River where Yenna used to bathe according to legends. The Grandik stemmed from the far north where icy blue glaciers engulfed mountains far above the clouds. Where ancient cities were said to have once been part of a famous route to the north, now lost to the ages.

"The river is high." Chase eyed the green-blue tinted water. "Do we wait? The supplies will never be able to get through that, if half of the soldiers even will."

"There can be no waiting. We are all running on shortened time," Alexander replied.

Alexander walked around the fires and checked on everyone after each day. He saw the pussy sores of gray and purple. It was impossible not to notice the grimaces from aching bones and muscles that burned with a thousand fires. All of them were being devoured from the inside by an invisible enemy.

"I need thirty of you with me. Horses too, and hold your shields tight against the current," Alexander told them.

Every man there would have stepped up. Time was an opponent and each one wanted to be free of it. Alexander seemed to invoke a sense of loyalty and they believed in him. They believed in the cause. In a matter of seconds thirty steeds sped into the water. Droplets flew in all directions as horses crashed against the current, battling to gain composure. Freezing water struck them with a shock. Goosepimples took over Alexander's skin and caused him to shiver.

"In a line!" Alexander commanded.

Confident riders turned their horses to stand against the current. The flow of water slowed immediately.

"Now cross!"

"Go! Go!" Timothy shouted.

"Don't stand there like lame ducks!" Adrian added.

They crossed with great haste behind the line of men holding shields against the unrelenting water. It battered the shields as it poured over onto those that held tight. As the last man rushed to the other side, the shield wall broke one at a time to not be swept away by the vicious water. Alexander let each soldier pass him as all eyes were on him. None would see him struggle, he had to hide how sore his muscles were, and how is hands had become numb. Muscular legs struggled against the current as the horse pushed through and moved up the slight hill where all awaited.

"First task complete." One corner of Alexander's mouth slanted upward. His eyes twinkled.

"They followed you without question, Alexander," Timothy

told him.

"That is a good sign. To do what we must, we will all have to work together."

6

VI

Weary Bones

Warhorses trudged on for days. All were saddle sore, but none would show it. Cooler temperatures during the nights made the days appear less difficult. Being able to cross the river and maintain all of their supplies made a positive beginning that many joked about. Morale was high as those trapped in Assin became free to roam once more. Everyone's body ached-no one was properly conditioned for the long ride. Their scabs flaked, oozing and tearing away at their flesh every time they moved. And still… After the daring escape at the river, an air of hopefulness reigned supreme throughout the camp.

The Olaria Mountains rose in front of them with snowcapped peaks. To their south was the quainter Wallar Kingdom. The gritty old king, known as Vlad Hembri, was a ruthless old man said to have seven wives. A strange thought for Alexander. One wife had been more than enough for him. More was a terrifying thought.

"We must have scouts out at all times until we cross here. Within days we will go through three lands," Alexander told them. "It will not be simple riding."

"Barbok Kingdom should be busy and will pay us no mind. They are on the front of many battles," Chase replied. "There is no way they have much for defensive measures in the west."

"Wallar has refused to do much in this war. Fearful cunts," Adrian snapped. "Wallarians are weak with blade and with heart."

"Our war isn't with them. We must stay on task," Alexander replied, then added, glaring at the older man, "You're very angry when you're not drunk."

"To the ends of the earth Yenna moved. The goddess brought food to feed those in need and war to those that suppressed. Light sparked from each step she took and shimmered off her mighty blade. Wolves sang to her in the night and birds in the day. Yenna walked to the edge of the earth to smooth out the enemy, to bury them, for evil cannot be allowed to stand," Timothy recited as his eyes gazed toward two chickadees that fought off a hawk above.

"Didn't know we were in bloody church," Adrian grumbled.

"Are we not? This is the church of the gods. Outdoors. Nature. They built this. A world for us. We march in their names. Each step we take, each day we breathe, the birds, the deer, the water, that is all created by them. Do you not believe?" Timothy pondered, searching for answers in Adrian's scruffy beard and dark eyes.

"Don't accuse me." Adrian pulled a dagger from his hip within a flash and held the point toward Timothy who didn't flinch or budge.

"Not an accusation. Just a question. Why does a question

cause you such anger?" the priest asked, not raising his voice, despite the sudden rise in tension.

"The gods have damned me." Adrian's lip twitched and he fidgeted with the dagger in his hand. "They stripped me of the few things I held dear. Sent me to a place to die without honor."

"Now they give you a chance to rise to glory." Timothy rested his hand over Adrian's as he clung to the hilt of the dagger. "You will find redemption, but you must repent. The gods give and the gods take; mere mortals should not question."

"Repent?!" Adrian twisted his head and spit to the side. "I prayed every day to the gods. I fought battles in their names. I sacrificed *everything*. Repent, you say." He pulled up his sleeve and revealed crackled gray skin and struggling veins. "My bones feel like they are being burned away. My skin turns gray and falls off. Wounds fester. Repent…" Adrian chugged from his bottle of liquor. "This is where I repent." He thrusted the dagger into the ground with his opposite hand.

Both Chase and Alexander only watched as the intense rhetoric turned into mumbles and more sips from the bottle. Timothy adjusted his shirt and eyed the drunken man.

Timothy adjusted his shirt. "You can drink away your pain, but it won't bring you to the gates of the heavens."

* * *

They swept south, below the mountains and through the Wallar kingdom. It was difficult to avoid the few forts that stood in the middle of vast openness and more difficult for the ones that stood on higher ground, but they ducked behind hills until they made it over another river into Alfrenia, a staunch ally of Sienna. Still, they did not want the four-hundred and four soldiers to be seen and had a long trek until they reached the border of Higania conquest. Using trees, to stick to the shadows, they rode horses through dense woods. Underbrush and thick branches hampering their way as they trudged forward.

"Last time I fought feels like an age ago." Alexander studied a scar on his arm where a blade once threatened to sever it from his body.

"I was only in two battles," Timothy replied.

"Two battles where you held fast and strong," Alexander added. "If I recall, you were the youngest among us and still you refused to yield. Many said you slayed hundreds on your own that day."

"Hundreds!" Adrian's laugh boomed like thunder as spit flung forward.

Timothy eyed him. "A bad day when Ventria fell to those heathens. A bad day." With a large sigh, he continued. "My best friend died that day. Russell of House Carroll of Yandale. An arrow to the calf and a sword to his back. I remember his blood stained face and the agonizing yell. Everything went silent as I watched, but his yell became louder. It threatened to burst my ears. He was a good lord. His father was a good lord. The Uleraks." The thought made Timothy shiver. "The way they used spears, those demon helmets. Vicious."

"Losing people is part of battle," Adrian responded. "I have seen thousands die, boys, women, elders, and cripples. Death seeks us all. It holds no favor."

"There is favor when you meet the gods," Alexander broke in.

"We hope," Chase said in a hushed tone. "I hope we don't see the Uleraks though."

VI

Each time they stopped, questions rattled off like arrows toward an enemy. Alexander had a difficult time appeasing each person aside from sheer optimism. On multiple occasions all four-hundred-four of them were forced to hide from any on the roads. Forests made for a longer journey, as did hills, but too often there was no choice. Any that realized they had Bentillux would be as likely to kill them as force them back. They were spotted along the Barbok border. Pointed helmets of the Alfrenian soldiers sped toward them with red tassels that drifted at the top. On their chest was the oak tree sigil of Alfrenia. Alexander held his hand up for the army to stop and many in the back dispersed into the woods. Each of the main four covered their faces with dark purple cloth.

Skidding to a stop, the horse dug its hooves in. A wide-eyed captain with a small nose eyed the group.

"Who are you?" he inquired.

"Some passerbys." Alexander clutched his reigns tight as his tanned fingers whitened.

"Why do you cover your faces? You have Bentillux?"

"We do," Alexander was honest.

Behind the captain men shifted on their horses with discomfort.

"Go back to where you came from then. Why do you threaten to spread it?" the captain snapped at them. "By the gods, you threaten the world!"

"Be silent," Alexander commanded. "We are going to war. Yes, we have the disease. It isn't as if you will catch it within an instant. Do not be naive. We will bring war to the enemy as a unit. Stay clear of us and do not worry. We will be gone from here before you know it. You have my word."

Teeth sunk into his lip as those large eyes studied them. Each of the soldiers in the opposite unit held firm as their eyes studied the massive group in front of them. Eyes of distrust and fear. Not only was Alexander's army larger but they were diseased men who sat horses too close for the comfort of the 'clean'. Tension rose between the small patrol unit and the army in front of them.

The captain studied him and grunted. "I hope you're being honest. Stay out of the villages. If I see you again within two days, I will have to have you killed. Two days." Then the captain took a wide sweep and the others trotted behind him.

"You have elephant-sized balls." Adrian laughed. "Huge."

"Praise be to Yenna." Timothy sighed.

"You are too young to be so anxious," Chase said.

"Just praising our goddess."

Alexander leaned down to where only Canyon could hear him. "I am thankful for you. Sorry you have to put up with them."

* * *

That evening Alexander spent a long time with Canyon. Brushing her mane, attending the mare's hooves, and scratching any spot that might itch.

"I am sorry I have brought you on such a long journey. I can't imagine it without you though. I trust you more than any other creature on this planet. I remember you has a baby. The moment you came out you wobbled but you had a drive, a spirit. It didn't take you long to run. Watching you grow…you are basically a child to me." His hand rubbed across her dark fur as she nudged him with her snout. "I am riding to my certain death, but I don't intend to let you die. When I am gone, run off into the sunset. Be free and fine love. Have babies and live a life in the countryside."

His back pressed against her muscular shoulder as he looked up into the sky where blue melted into purple that faded with the sun.

* * *

"There's a battle ahead. We have reached Zurkey," Chase said.

Beyond them, steel on steel screeched with high pitches. Shouts of death and life sliced through the noise of battle. A symphony of sword, death, and the struggle to live.

"We made good time. They are below the hill?"

"Yes, in a pitched battle."

"Then let us make an entrance none will forget. One that that plays will be created for. Bards will sing our songs. This will be our first showing to the world of who we are. This will be the beginning of how they will remember us."

Instead of the sigh he wanted to release, Chase smiled at his brother.

"Are you all ready?" Alexander asked.

"With Yenna's blessing," Timothy replied.

Adrian rolled his eyes and grunted.

"On me!" Alexander commanded.

The command to follow Alexander echoed down the lines. They separated into units of fifty with few gaps between them.

Silver armor was donned, with the snakes on the chest and shin greaves. Wind whipped blue cloaks as they streamed down the hillside as one unit. Horses dug in, sending a dirt cloud above them.

Below, horns sounded and each side stared toward the arrival of a new force, unfamiliar to each of them. Questions were sure to fill the fray of battle from the two armies already in the heat of battle, but Alexander had no time for that. Leading them in a curve, they sped toward the golden armored infantry of Higania with their banners of five hawks. The leaders had purple plumes that stood upon their helmets. Blue fluttered among the hill and caused the green hill to swell like the sea.

Thunder erupted as the new force swarmed the field toward the Higanians, Alexander first. Soldiers from Sienna reminded Alexander of who he used to be. One of them, long ago, before they sent him to rot in Assin. Underneath his horse a soldier collapsed into a heap of death, while his sword struck in multiple directions. Severing life from body, Alexander swung with a new found vigor. It was the first time in so long he had felt truly alive, watching his enemies eyes glaze with death. Spears and swords struck at Alexander, but metal rang upon metal each time he blocked them. Like the sea, blue cloaks swallowed golden armor, tossing them and churning them into a red tide.

Those with the blue cloaks hunted the enemy with their symbol of five hawks, believed to be a symbol of their supposed, mighty god. Alexander found a man with a large red plume showing him to be a commander. Standing on his horse, he leapt and tackled the man. Both men landed with thuds as they tumbled across the ground, entangled with one another. Alexander ended up on the bottom of the other with a harrowing pain in his ribs from impact. There was no time to focus on injury. A sword thrusted at his face. He dodged, barely. The side of the blade left a slight nick upon his cheek. Using his hips to press upward, he managed to flip the other man over. Alexander yanked a dagger from his hip before his opponent could raise his sword. Cold steel penetrated the warm throat. Eyes widened with surprise and the man went limp. All around Alexander, the enemy lay dead. The city of Zurkey was delivered from being annexed thanks to the arrival of Alexander and the others. Overhead, grey clouds swirled, waging their own battle against the vibrant blue.

Beside him, Chase and Timothy helped sweep away the enemy with fine strokes and speed. Alexander peered back to see if any of his followers had fallen. It appeared that they hadn't, but it was difficult to know in the midst of chaos. Sienna soldiers stood holding watchful gazes and wide eyes of surprise. All of the sick made sure to avoid those from Sienna, but upon the Higanians they let out their frustration in strokes that dealt death across the field.

Higanian infantry had moved behind their lines from the other side to stop the bleeding but were quick to be routed. Brave faces fought on doggedly but were forced to flee or fall forever.

"Give chase!" Alexander waved them on.

Battles are to be had everywhere.

"They are coming." Chase pointed.

"We must ride." Alexander sprinted to his horse and set off at a gallop with the others behind him, leaving confusion in their wake.

Once they were far enough away, they made camp.

"Invigorating! It feels so good to be alive. Almost makes you forget the pain inside!" Alexander set his helmet down and dipped his face in the small stream, washing dried blood from his cheeks and chin.

"Did you see their faces?" Adrian shouted as he ran into the water. "Fear. They feared us. We brought death upon the miserable cunts! Bloody the field and cut off the hand! It's good to be alive!" Blood covered the man like a blanket.

Unlike the other three, Timothy sat by the water and rubbed water on himself with slow and methodical movements. Every inch of blood needed to be taken from him.

"What are you doing?" Chase eyed him.

"It is the blood of death. Give it to the gods, the fish, or the crows. I do not want it staining me. I do what I must, it does not mean I must enjoy it. May the gods accept this at their hands and deem me worthy or unworthy by their own accord. Praise be to Yenna. Praise be to Bevelon. Praise be to Leve."

Chase watched the man as blue, liquid eyes reflected the water in front of them.

7

VII

Battle of Ravens

The next three days were full of small skirmishes. Constant evasion of Sienna's scouts made an annoying task for Alexander and his followers.

"We must claim a name for ourselves," Alexander said.

"Sea of Snakes," Chase said.

"Not that," Timothy replied. "How about the Order of Fate?"

Each of the other three eyed him with smiles, well Adrian a faint smirk, but that was as much joy as the man got aside from death and alcohol.

"That is a respectable name. The Order of Fate," Alexander said.

"Even I can't argue it." Adrian took a large swig, then belched in Timothy's face.

"Classy."

"Do we have a battle plan?" Chase asked.

"This one will not be a battle. It will be a massacre in the name of Yenna."

"Tonight is Jennia," Timothy added. "Should we not feast and be pleasant for our goddess? It is our faith to do such."

"I almost forgot about that. Praise be to Yenna. We can deliver our enemy's blood and then feast," Alexander replied. "We will give her the greatest honor. Yenna understands. Has she not blessed us herself? Look at the number we have sent to their grave in her name."

"At least Leve's earth can partake," Timothy sighed. "Two gods feasting at once. How could you all forget?"

"What do you question so?" Alexander eyed the younger man.

Blue eyes flashed up at him. "I question much, Alexander. I question a great many things. I will hold my pact and my honor, the little I have left. Without questioning we are blind, but we do not question the gods."

"We need to fuck," Adrian interrupted.

"You are not much my type, Adrian." Alexander smirked.

"Women, you cunt. I want to fuck a woman. A man from time to time is fine as well, but I have had that. I need to toss a woman in the midst."

"Must you?" Timothy snapped.

"Must I fuck a woman? Yes. If you want a man, there are plenty of those, but many of them have already had me so you'll just disappoint."

"I don't fuck men."

"Then women it is I guess."

"No."

"Wait, are you a virgin?" Chase's eyes grew as large as two moons.

A deep shade of red consumed the younger man's face and clashed with his vibrant blue eyes.

"A bloody virgin!" Adrian slapped his leg as laughs erupted from his large chest. "A virgin! You've never touched the nectar of the gods then."

"I will when I reach the gates. I was saving myself for the one," Timothy attempted to explain. "My mate of the soul. My true love."

"The one?" Adrian all but fell over as he wheezed and choked.

"Come on." Alexander shoved the larger, drunker man. "I haven't slept with anyone since I was forced away from my wife. I could never touch another woman."

"He's never even touched one though. Boy would probably blast himself if he saw a tit."

"You are a vulgar man," Timothy replied. "A disgusting, vulgar man."

A large hand slapped against Timothy's shoulder as Adrian leaned in laughing.

"I think tonight, I will fuck a woman in your honor."

"Less about fucking. We will attack soon. It is dark. We will be like wolves in the night."

"Wolves also fuck," Adrian's laughter boomed like beats of a war drum.

* * *

Horses were tied up and left behind as the Order of Fate crept in silence under the thin slice of pale moon with shadows of clouds swallowing it and spitting it out. Black figures crept around the well-lit camp full of laughs, sex, and games.

For a large man, Adrian was swift, even with the cracked

skin and aching muscles. Grabbing hold of a guard, he cranked his neck with a quick snap, then lay him on the ground. Four-hundred-four men circled the massive camp in units of ten. A high-pitched bird call from Chase signaled the attack. The troops poured in from all angles like a flash flood. Blades of spears and swords ripped through tents. Blood sprayed where swords split skin, regardless of whether their victims were pissing, having sex, or sleeping. Timothy was the only one who refused to kill.

Alexander grabbed the younger man by the cloak that draped across his chest.

"You have to kill, if one of them comes awake it could be a dagger in any of our backs because you refused to kill them in their sleep," he growled.

"It lacks honor. I refuse to kill people while they dream." Timothy grabbed Alexander's wrists and pushed them down.

"There are worse ways to go." Alexander turned to do what he must.

Through a tent they moved like shadows of death as fires outside illuminated their silhouettes. His dagger slid against throats and plunged into chests. Men woke, wide-eyed just to fall back to eternal sleep with gasps, hands outstretched in horror. Shouts erupted all over the camp as the enemy attempted to rally. Chaos ensued. Those who were positioned outside the camp cut down any that moved their way. Feet splashed in blood, alcohol, and piss as soldiers clashed. Unprepared Higanians were cut down from the side, front, and back.

"Heathen cunts!" Adrian pulled his blade from one's lower back. "Taste my steel. Lick it and love it." Wheeling around, his sharp blade sliced into an upcoming soldier's ribs.

Ashes pelted Alexander's face as the man he cut down fell

into a fire in front of them, screaming flesh burned and left a grotesque stench in the air. Sweat consumed the skin under Alexander's armor as reckless blades swung toward him, the metal glowing red from fire. Alexander rolled to the ground, then thrust his blade upward into the man's ribs. Another blade slashed by his cheek. Without another option, he smashed his head against his attacker's face. Blood gushed from the man's nose and Alexander finished him with a clean swipe.

To his side, he saw his brother topple over with two soldiers in front of him. There was no time to waste as dozens of tents erupted into flame. Sprinting over, Alexander kicked the first soldier in the side and sent him into the other. Being focused in a swordfight was the difference between life and death. Anticipating each moment and being prepared for what could happen were all parts of the dance. The first swung at Alexander. He spun him off and landed the horse-head pommel against the second's face with a loud crack. Then turning back, his sword caused the other's head to sway to the side as his neck opened up. Chase was on the ground breathing heavily next to the dead soldier.

"Come on, brother. No time to lay down. Too much death to be dealt." Alexander reached out his hand and pulled his brother up.

"Mhmm. Funny. Watch your left." Chase thrust at a rushing enemy.

Around them, swords and spears blended like a symphony with shrieks and cries of death. Shouts in another language filled the air more. Blue cloaks were easy to spot as many moved together, pinning soldiers between them. Some looked defeated, but when you trapped a mouse, even a mouse fought back. Sensitive skin under the armor burned. Bones cried under the weight of the armor and at any impact. There was no time to focus on the pain, death was in front of Alexander.

"Shields!"

Rectangle shields swung in front of each soldier. They stepped in unison and pushed the defenders back against one another. Spears and swords struck through gaps of the shields while others glanced off with heavy thuds. Dead bodies clung to feet with each step as more of the enemy became pressed between shield and sword.

"Cut them down. None will survive today. A feast for the crows and a feast for Yenna. You have come too far, tell your god to fall at our knees. Pray for forgiveness if you must. Your time is done," Alexander told them.

Shrieks erupted and cries for mercy, for their mothers, and then unintelligible words and phrases as sword and spear struck the blows of death. Body upon body dropped until the very last one fell to his knees with eyes to the sky.

Adrian stepped forward and looked down at him.

"There is nothing up there for you, cunt." He eyed the man's armor that presented him as some lord with the sigil and all of the honorific badges on his shoulders. With a mighty swing, the man's head severed and tumbled into the sea of blood and body parts.

Adrian picked up the head and glared into the deadened eyes. "I just want to watch the life drain from your eyes."

"Victory!" Alexander shouted.

Everyone chanted in elation. Even Timothy joined in the chaotic tones as ravens flocked to a midnight feast. They killed men in their sleep. There wasn't honor to be found in it, but there was necessity. Alexander had to make peace with that.

The army cheered as they moved back to the tent. Six of the

dead were carried, but only six. An entire camp of at least two thousand was dead below. A blow to the numbers of Higania and a stroke of pride for the Order of Fate.

"Alexander!" one soldier shouted.

"Ave Sanctus Imperator!" another came.

"Alexander, Sanctus Imperator!" the phrase was echoed.

"Sanctus Imperator?" Chase pulled his brother close. "That is heresy. If the emperor heard it he would."

"Kill me?" Alexander shrugged. "I am a dead man regardless. We are all dead men here. Whatever honor they want to give, let them. Men need something to fight for."

"Okay, Sanctus Imperator." Chase said sarcastically, shaking his head.

"I do not deserve such a title." Alexander waved his hand to quiet the crowd. "If you wish to bestow it upon me, then I will humbly accept it at your hands."

Cheers spouted like geysers and bloodied fists pumped into the air. Swept upward, Alexander sat on Adrian's broad shoulders.

"I hope the gods do not dim his light too soon," Timothy told Chase.

"We will see. I hope the gods are good."

"Gods are not so simple, my friend. They aren't necessarily good or bad. They are beyond our comprehension."

* * *

"Have you ever been in love?" Chase asked Timothy. "I know you haven't, *you know*, but have you ever loved anyone?"

"I have only ever loved the gods." Timothy poked a stick in the fire. "There was a woman my father wanted me to marry. A girl from House Hendrilla. Pretty, slender legs, and locks of auburn hair. Lords don't always get to love; we get to do what is right for our house."

"I was in love once." Adrian's glared into the fire as if he saw someone's face within it.

"You were?" Chase's jaw slacked. "Truly?"

Breath exhaled with a vast sigh. "Heathria Nell. The most beautiful woman I had ever seen. Curves to make a man go mad." He bit into his knuckle. "Eyes like melted honeypots and lips like feather pillows. A commanding woman, a power, and no fear." Adrian laughed at the thought. "One time she battered me so that you would have thought I got in a fight with two bears. Sex with her, that was the fiercest battle I ever had."

"What happened?" Timothy inquired.

"Turned out she had a husband."

For the first time, true sadness swelled in Adrian's eyes, threatening to douse the fire with a rainstorm.

"He found out?"

"I found out. I asked her and she told me that we just were having fun. I…begged her to leave him. She laughed in my face. I could have killed him. Could have killed her too. Instead, I vowed to never love again. A stupid emotion. I enjoy a good fuck and killing fills me with joy. I need nothing else." There was silence around the fire. Pain cracked the hard man's face.

Love. Entienne. Those beautiful eyes, that hair—the way she would gasp each time he penetrated her. Nights of looking at the stars, discussing their future. How many times had they promised forever? Never again to lock fingers. Never again to feel the sweet kiss of pure ecstasy.

Alexander hoped she would love again, but the very thought made his stomach sicken, swelling in knots. She deserved to love, even if he could not.

What cruelty—to make it so one must perish because he can't touch his love ever again. Only the gods know. Only you three gods know. I do this for you, but it comes at such a high cost. Entienne.

* * *

Two days later, another small battle was one with only wounded, none killed on their side. A third, decisive victory where Alexander employed the pincer movement that worked with perfection. A claw like a crab's, a pincer of death that collapsed the army that attempted to stand against them. Then brown mountains stood in front of them, bathed in violet light of the early morning. Either the gods were on Alexander's side or death wasn't prepared for any that followed him.

Alexander stood in the middle of the army. "Up there is Ebora. It was once a great mountain city until the Higanians stormed it and seized it in a four-month battle. The city was starved and forced to eat their own in hopes of salvation that never came. We will liberate the city. Free it of the oppressors. Are you with me?"

"Ave Sanctus Imperator!" Sword hilts clanged against shields.

Up the mountain pass they moved. Small ants that strolled between large peaks on each side. Red and brown, dry rock that fell often with loud thunder down the mountains leaving trails of dust in its wake.

"We wait here until the early morning." Alexander stopped the force of three-hundred ninety-eight. Some almost fell from their horses either from exhaustion or sheer pain. "There is a gate ahead. We storm it before the sun has risen and then charge to the city two miles beyond. Before the sun begins to beat down upon us."

Many washed at rotted skin, while others rubbed stinging muscles that caused for stiff movement.

Sleep was difficult to come by. Pressure now rested upon Alexander's shoulders. The journey of death had resulted in much more glory than anticipated. Beside him, Adrian snored with a bottle at his side, Chase curled into a ball, and Timothy sat up in prayer. Alexander as always protected his younger brother. Now, he looked at his wavy hair as he slept, he had brought him to assured death. Somehow, he managed to look peaceful. There were worse ways to die. Arms ached as if hammered by a blacksmith as Alexander rubbed them, especially in spots of greyed skin, hard as leather.

"Better get sleep if you wish to lead in the name of the gods tomorrow," Timothy spoke without opening his eyes. "Looking into the face of death is the only time you truly know what life means."

"Sleep will come soon," Alexander replied. "There is much to do first."

Timothy laid down and covered up with his cloak.

"Rest."

Alexander made sure each night everyone beat their cloaks clean. That would be how people remembered them.

Red, like the glow of a forge, split the horizon in a line as the sun began its journey to the sky. Alexander stood and stared east, waiting for the moment to arouse the army. Silence held a beauty, a peace that he desired to soak in. Few were awake as if they could not wait to face death or glory once more. Winning was contagious and invigorating, there was no doubt about that as men woke, donning their armor without a word. Alexander clung to hope that the gods would favor them once more, even though he knew all they could count on was each other.

Admiral blue stood out against the red and brown rocks around them, but their horses charged upward. The enemy could see death coming, but their foresight wouldn't change the outcome. Only four men manned the arched stone gate and were trampled over before they knew what was happening. Hooves pounded against stone, the very earth beneath them trembled as if ready to cave in, and the Order of Fate sped forward prepared for battle.

They say the moment you seek glory is the moment you fall. Is there ever true prestige in death? Being remembered there is glory, but if those you love do not venerate you, what does it matter if strangers know your name? Entienne, my love. I hope you think fondly upon me. Even to death, your face is all I can see.

Clatter of armor snapped Alexander back as his horse toppled over an unsuspecting defender. The walls of the city connected to the brown mountains. Formed stone hitting against jagged stones that stretched upward. Shouts on the wall were followed by figures sprinting around to grab their bows. Before Alexander and his followers knew, arrows fell from the bright blue sky, but the gate was not fully closed. Shields raised in defense. Digging his heels into his steed, Alexander pressed on while the others followed. Arrows clanged against the Order of Fate and dropped to the ground to be trampled underfoot and hoof. An arrow tore through Alexander's blue cloak and another bounced off the snake head pauldron.

Funneling through the massive gates, the Order of Fate

hacked and slashed at the guards before the two separate doors could slam shut. More defenders pushed through the crowd as civilians ran in all directions in a chaotic frenzy. Arrows fell in all directions, but now blue cloaks and silver armor meshed with red and gold.

Timothy's horse reared, a hoof concaving a soldier's helmet, and still the younger man swung his sword with great poise. Graceful slashes of the younger warrior caused him to look untouchable as his steed moved side-to-side and swung around in swift whirls. Battles inside of a city were a different beast, much more complicated than pitched battles, but the element of surprise was on their side. With their slow responses, it was clear the defenders did not anticipate a battle.

A sea of gold and red were in front of Alexander and his army, but many of them were still attempting to adjust their armor with anxious fingers. Blue cloaks and horses parted the mass of Higanians and soon the locals, who were in the service of their captives, flipped sides. Any weapon the locals could find was raised up against their oppressors. Arrows struck thigh, arm, and neck of the Higanians. Shouts of salvation echoed through the city as Alexander continued to slice his way through the enemy. "Pay attention!" Chase's sword struck a soldier's neck. "No time to daydream, brother!" Chase continued onward with Alexander following him.

As kids, the two had practiced together often, pretending it was them against the world. In real battles, they had put it to the test time after time. Now for the final time, the brothers could wage battle next to one another. It brought a smile to Alexander's face. "It is getting too tight for the horses." Alexander slid off his mount as his soldiers filtered in around him.

VII

Gold armor shimmered down the tight alleys in retreat.

"Two hundred of you stay with the horses and guard this gate. The rest, with me! Let's go Canyon."

Into the fray they moved—Chase, Timothy, Adrian, and others at Alexander's back. Through each alley, they swept clean the enemy with vicious strikes from their blades. They sped toward the center where an acropolis stood with large marble columns. Once there were three statues of each god in the acropolis, now the heads were torn from them. Anger burned inside of Alexander at the thought of them beheading the gods, a rage that urged him forward. *Thrust, parry, riposte, thrust.* His blade struck its target while he managed to evade any blows that moved toward him. Shoulder to shoulder, the two brothers defended each blow, and struck out with speed. Sweat filled Alexander's arms, his chest heaved, and his wrist grew tired, but on he moved. The ache of his bones, the sores in his skin, made moving more difficult than it was before. Last time Alexander battled, he was the epitome of health.

Timothy moved with grace, almost as a dancer with a sword in his hand. He wasn't even sweating. Dodging, then grappling, but none could get a hand on him before he sent them to the afterlife. Then his foot slammed against an enemy's chest, followed by a sweeping cut. Slashes with great speed sent the enemy to their death. Blades whirled overhead as he ducked under and with a quick thrust, his sword found its target once again.

Adrian on the other hand fought with raw power. The larger man overwhelmed his enemy with a brutal onslaught. Overhead swings and swipes that could sever a horse's head overpowered those he targeted. Sweat ran from under his helmet down his face, causing his cheeks to glisten in the sun.

Still the darker man ravaged the enemy like a cat upon a rabbit hole.

Brown stone was covered in bodies, with cracks that swelled with blood. All around the acropolis lay bodies of the enemy. Tattered and worn down, the locals hailed the soldiers as saviors with shouts of glee. Old, young, and all in between, haled them as heroes.

"Mother, may you and the other gods accept this sacrifice. All around you is the death of those who defiled the three. We lay them at your feet. Deliver us from evil." Timothy's arms stretched outward as a bird prepared to take flight. "Someone write this: *For today you are saved. Ebora will rise once more. In Yenna's name, you are delivered!*"

"He does have a way with words," Chase said.

Alexander smiled and nodded.

"Remember the Order of Fate. For we fight in Yenna's honor. We fight for her! You must stay back for yes, we have Bentillux. We shall leave you now. Do not get too close to us with the blue cloaks. Know that we bring death where we go."

Some of the cheers dwindled, but many others seemed not to care. All they saw was a liberated city, their faith, their freedom re-installed. Adrian dove into a bar and ran out with two large bottles.

"For Yenna." He shrugged.

It took time to move the horses and supply wagons to the other side of the city. The entire city was full of narrow streets and winding paths, but the eastern gate was wide open. Upon the wall they still cheered for the heroes. Some of the fallen laid upon a wagon of death, ten. Three-hundred-eighty-eight blue cloaks still fluttered with life. More than Alexander would have anticipated. Numbers dwindled, but they would never be forgotten. Each name and date of death was written by Timothy in a brown leather book.

"Every person must be remembered. Every name must be counted," Timothy said each time another entry was made, followed by, "Praise be to Yenna."

"We are getting closer to Solaria," Alexander said.

"We are." Chase nodded.

That evening they sat around a fire toward the bottom of the mountains. Adrian's meaty hand smashed against Timothy's back with a guffaw.

"What is wrong with you?!" Timothy shouted. "Brains turned to slush with that poison you drown yourself in. That is Hell's piss and you sip on it so gingerly."

"Gingerly?" One of Adrian's dark eyes squinted. "Don't be such a little girl. *Hell's piss.* Maybe you should drink some, aye?" Thick fingers wrapped around Timothy's neck. "You act as if I am sucking the cock of the underworld. I sip upon the nectar of the gods, boy."

"Stop!" Alexander jumped up and grabbed Adrian's rope-tough forearm.

"Just having some fun. We are dying and you all are so sensitive," Adrian laughed, shoving Alexander backward.

A few eyes turned toward them but quickly snapped back to what they were doing.

"Just because we are dying doesn't mean we have to be idiots." Timothy stood up with blue eyes turned fierce and shoved the much larger man.

"You want to do this?" Adrian smirked.

Hands pressed against his large chest, but the man seemed unmoved aside from a small drunken stagger.

"Let's do it then."

Before Adrian's haymaker made it all the way around, Timothy's fist landed against the bigger man's throat. A lightning quick kick to the knee and then as Adrian dropped, a strike against his cheek rendered him unconscious.

"Stupid drunk. Now you can rest and so can we." Timothy sat down with both sets of eyes on him. "What?"

"Nothing." Chase laughed. "Nothing at all."

8

VIII

Apathy of Death

One soldier had succumbed to death in the night with a bout of coughing that sent blood from his mouth. Going out on a massive victory. Eternal slumber would be found under rocks at the foot of the mountain as the two closest to him kneeled and prayed. Others followed and did the same to pay respect. Alexander took a deep breath.

Another one dead. This one not in battle. Tragedy.

"Did you knock me out last night?" Adrian rubbed his head.

"I did," came Timothy's curt reply.

"Only because I was drunk. Otherwise, it would never have happened."

"I can do it again right now if you'd like." Timothy's blue eyes gazed forward, not paying Adrian much attention.

"Maybe tomorrow. My head hurts." Adrian continued to rub his thick, matted hair.

"I am always open to it."

All Alexander could do was shake his head at the two. There were still hundreds of miles between Solaria and Ebora. By now there were sure to be troops everywhere sent to root out the army that had liberated too much land from the empire in such a minimal time.

"Elite units are guaranteed to come now." Alexander told them. "To this point we have only seen standard soldiers, there is no way that continues."

"Why do you say that?" Chase asked.

"We have won too much. It is certain that they take this threat seriously now."

Rain drizzled upon them, much needed to clean armor and skin alike. None seemed to be bothered as they continued onward through the day of light drizzle that cleansed them. They held their heads high even though inside their bodies were battling against them. Now they all realized there was no going back. Death was inevitable, their sores, their bones, and their wounds all festered. Friends had died along the way and they were all signed to death as well.

Timothy began to sing.

"I was trained in the hand of the light
   There will be no darkness for me tonight.
   Yenna's hands hold me tight
   If I am to die, let me die in a holy fight,
   Do not succumb to the darkness
   For waking hours bring forth new promise,
   Evil always attempts to devour
   To you with blood we pay homage.
   Brothers and sisters, swords ringing like bells
   Peace comes at a cost

Sickened are those who stand in the stomach of Hell
Not all who wander are lost."

A deep voice echoed in the drizzle as all listened. Throughout two days the constant showers continued, wetness sinking into their bones. Dampness caused wounds to become to damp and sensitive skin to become irritated. It was impossible not to shiver, but Alexander forced himself to hold his head high through the gray soaked sky and muddy ground. There was no doubt about exhaustion, but none would let it override their pride.

"Did you hear that?" someone asked a few feet off.

"People?" Chase attempted to whisper. With eyes squinted and water that dripped over them like film, he could make out the crest of red horse hair. "Do you see the red?" Chase leaned over. "I think it is them."

"Enemy! Charge!" Alexander commanded.

Without much visibility, Alexander led them forward. None hesitated; hesitation resulted in death. A melee of dancing horses splashed water in all directions, while swords slipped in wet hands and the battle commenced. Silver masks with horns stepped forward with long spears, tied with red ribbon like demons.

"Uleraks!" Alexander shouted.

Spears thrusted through the gray veil, some striking armor with clings, and others finding flesh of horse or man. Shrieks of pain stemmed from both sides, eerie in the gray soaked air that hung all around them. Clinging to vibrant blue cloaks like a ghost, the wetness seemed heavy upon them. Ulerak spears dashed in and out with precision and speed.

"Focus on breaking their spears!" Alexander shouted. "Cut

through the wood!"

Easier said than done, as red ribbon flashed by his face. Water mixing with the blood from the gash now on his cheek, it ran down toward his armor as if trying to escape.

A spear shot toward Chase's face. It splintered with a crack as he managed to break the spear point off before it could be retracted. All around him screams flooded through the drizzle. The demonesque attacker fell as Chase's sword sliced neck flesh. Water trickled off the silver mask that stared into the mud.

"Stay together!" Alexander spotted a few soldiers who drifted apart in the misty battle.

Following admiral blue cloaks seemed easy, but it was also easy for the enemy spears that struck out like serpents.

We are the snakes here, not you.

"Trample them." Alexander kicked at his horse. "Stomp them into the mud."

The command was echoed throughout the lines by others. It took a moment for the read to follow the lead, but they managed to all the same. Spears penetrated horses, sending them tumbling with whinnies, and splashes upon the ground as they flopped and kicked toward the air. The only option for the Order of Fate was to press forward. Swords swung as the horses trampled over the masked Uleraks that still struck out with vigorous thrusts. It was impossible to keep tabs on where everyone was.

All Alexander could do was fight and lead his army to victory or death. In front of him spears flashed through the fog. That was the danger of leading from the front, but leading from the back didn't inspire soldiers. That was what they came for—to deal death to the enemy. Perhaps it clouded his mind, all of the victories. A vision of something grander, standing atop the capital of the enemy empire. A notion that none of them were likely to see, but Alexander refused to not dream as his sword cut through the vapors and caused red to spray into the never-ending grayness.

An eerie silence marked the end of battle. Strange demon masks filled the muddy ground. Spears began to sink into the mud and the shrieks of battle and screeches of metal subsided. Only the sound of the wounded groaning or weeping.

In the end, it was impossible to know how many were dead on the mud filled field. All they could do was continue on and make it to their goal. Timothy would add the names later as he walked through the camp. Saddle sore and hungry, they were forced to stop for the rest of the day. The weather finally cleared as the sun broke through the mist and allowed them to fully count their casualties.

"Down to three-hundred-twenty-eight," Timothy reported. "We won but lost many left to drown in the mud with only the gods to watch over them." Blue eyes looked over pages of neatly written names.

There was nothing to say. A victory was a victory, but dwindling numbers meant more of an issue. Sorrow swelled inside of Alexander. They knew what they were getting into, but it didn't make it less difficult. Knowing they were somewhere, swallowed by the earth, with no one to send them off with love. They needed to reach the ancient city; there was no other option.

"Look at this gash. Right through my leathered skin." Adrian pointed to his bicep. "Fuckers got me. Ah, they got you too. That's a good scar." He pointed to Alexander's face. "That'll look fierce in the afterlife.

"Almost took my eye out."

"So, we live another day, aye. Glory is ours once more."

"Many fell today though," Chase replied.

"We came to die." Adrian took a drink. "They fell fighting."

"Give me some of that." Alexander reached out. "Take away some of this pain at least."

"Numb the pain and ease the mind. I am glad to be at your sides."

"We are glad to have you." Raising the bottle, Alexander chugged down multiple sips that caused all of their eyes to span wide.

"Slow down or you won't wake up until next week," Adrian laughed.

"There you are. Finally." A soldier with Sienna's armor on, with the green side cape and the sigil of the golden sun walked up toward them. "The blue death, they are calling you. The enemy that is. Some of ours are calling you Harbingers of Yenna along with some other names."

"Don't come closer," Alexander cautioned. "We are sick, please."

"I am Captain Dannilon Galphus. Bentillux?" He stopped ten feet away.

"Yes. All of us. We left Sinna to battle the enemy instead of die stuck inside those walls."

"And you are?"

"Alexander Riagani."

"I know that name. I was with you at the Battle of Carphalla. A good battle it was. Soldiers rallied around you, including myself. You could have commanded from the back, but you plunged into battle. Fought our way out of being surrounded. Soldiers that have nothing to lose, fighting to destroy Higania. That is a tale for an epic."

"That battle was rough. Many fell that day," Alexander recalled.

"They did," Dannilon replied. "My brother and two of my good friends."

"I am sorry for that," Alexander said.

"You saved many more. That battle at Zurkey. I wanted to thank you. I have followed you, everywhere you go is liberated. Sienna and others send more troops in to reinforce the areas you have taken back. Everyone owes you. They have sent more units out, but we have been able to sweep some away in recent days."

"I just want my wife and son to be proud."

"I will make sure they know of every feat. My soldiers will trail behind you if you have any need. We will guard your flank."

"Too close and they will get sick. We will march Solaria. We will hit them where the lands meet. With that gone, their seat of power in the west will collapse."

"Solaria, that is a brave task. May Yenna's fortune shine upon you all."

With that he was gone, back from where he came.

"Did you hear those names they call us?" Chase laughed.

"Perhaps we will be remembered after all," Adrian said.

"You want to be remembered?" Timothy raised his eyebrows in surprise.

"Don't we all? I still have desire. I drown my sorrow in the bottle like you drown yours in scripture. Maybe Yenna damns me for it, but this pain inside my body. The fevers, the cracking bones, the sores. The loss of everything I knew and loved. I drown myself and I am glad I do. If I didn't, I would be much more cruel."

Those blue eyes studied the larger man as if he was seeing

him for the first time.

"I want to be remembered for something good. I was cast off like we all were, to rot in Sinna and be forgotten."

"I…I'm sorry." Timothy's gaze moved toward the ground. "I didn't think about that. I just thought…"

"That I am an alcoholic and an ass. I know what you thought. I know what everyone thinks."

"Well, now you are my brother. Until we die and after." Timothy's hand stretched toward the other.

Eyeing it, Adrian reached out and grabbed it. "Until we die and after. A bond beyond life itself."

"It is an honor to fight at your side."

"Finally," Alexander broke in. "Too close to falter now. Soon we will face what we have come so far for."

* * *

Over the course of a week, three battles took place with only a small number of dead. As their number dwindled, the bond of Alexander's army grew stronger. Grizzled war veterans, each one with swords that dealt numerous deaths and eyes that remembered those that had fallen at their side. Stories were shared about the fallen, about their pasts, and of course, boasts of their kills. That was one way that soldiers filled the pain and remembered the dead. It also kept their spark alive. One of the battles was against the Hejars from the far east. Short warriors with great speed with and without their slender swords. Adrian demolished thirty of them himself. Their swords bent under his force and their light armor stood little chance against the onslaught. Supplies ran low until a shipment from Sienna was sent to them with a letter.

"You are all heroes of Sienna. We owe you a great debt and our gratitude. What you have given the world is hope. You will be remembered. For that, the least we can do is send you these supplies. Please take them. Fight bravely. May the gods bless you." – The King

A cart of vast foods and jars of milk, water, and even bottles of liquor were hitched to large horses.

"A present from the king. Incredible." Chase gawked along with the others. "Who knew we would have to just sacrifice ourselves to get some recognition. There is another letter. It is from…your wife."

Alexander snatched it and stared in disbelief before he opened it.

"Dearest Alexander, I am sorry that on our last meeting it went so terribly. I do not wish you to go on this journey thinking you are not loved. You have always been a burning star. One with great fire, great ambition, and power. I love you as I did twenty years ago when I first laid eyes on you. Those warrior eyes and that smile of kindness. I will love you for the rest of my life. At least you are not rotting away in some city. You are doing what you were born to do. Our son loves you as well. We speak of you often. Now I am able to tell him you are a hero. I received word from a captain about you and your endeavor. You are an honorable man. I hope this finds you still alive and I am sure it will. Killing you has never proven easy to any, even Bentillux. I hold you dear to my heart and our son will always know of you. I will never let your name fade away. You are

a hero; you are my love.
  With all adoration,
  Your wife."

Tears stung his eyes as they poured without him even realizing. To his knees he dropped in front of all, clutching the letter to his chest. No words were uttered; there was too much respect for the man. It took a few minutes as memories flashed through his mind. Now he could die with her love at hand. Inside of him the spark of love struck like lightning to a tree, a new fire. As he rose, so did the chant.

"Sanctus Imperator! Sanctus Imperator!" Swords rose to the sky.

"To death we march!" Alexander shouted. "First we feast."

Cheeses, bread, meat, fruit, vegetables, and wine were passed out to everyone. A feast fit for royalty as the remaining warriors ate as if it would be their last. How many cities had they liberated? How many people could venture back to their farms? To their homes? Alexander watched each man bite into food with joy, regardless of their discomfort.

"I would like to say a word." Timothy stood. "Matria tells us that Yenna is graceful and kind, even in dealing death. Not that she is not powerful, there is a poise to her vengeance.

"For seek ye, the favor of the mother goddess, under her all things are possible. A grace unlike any other with a passion and a power. With her mighty blade she deals death like fluid water. One second calm, the next a mighty swell that drowns the evil of the world. What beauty she holds, what radiance she is. Yenna is wise and knows when to strike. Bold moves are favored, as she likes when the fire burns hot at the time it must."

"Now is our time. We burn hot. We feed the hands of the gods. In her name we pray. All praise to Yenna."

"All praise to Yenna," they echoed.

"What is the plan then?" Chase asked.

"The plan is to die surrounded by dead Higanians. We will storm the walls and make it to the citadel. We can't die before then. That will be a show of strength."

"So, there is no actual plan?" Chase squinted at his brother.

"To kill as many of them as we can. I will find stairs and we will take to the wall. The streets won't do us much good, but the wall we can fight on."

9

IX

Fate is Fate

Through tall grasses that swayed in the gentle breeze, they approached with caution. Each of their bodies felt as if they had been battered by hammers. Muscles became refined from battles and riding, but it didn't stop the ache underneath. One of Alexander's wounds from Bentillux broke open as he crawled, causing him to bite his lip. A camp outside of the ancient city. Many said Solaria was the birthplace of the world where gods created humans. A city so old, so powerful, so important. The emperor knew that the land lost in the past few months had been crucial. Many of his men had been killed at the hand of the Order of Fate. Within two days they had captured six different patrols and left them as fertilizer for the earth.

"Do we have a plan?" Chase asked.

"I am thinking. I believe I have one, but I do not know how it will end."

"It all ends here regardless, right? I am at your side for any of it. I suppose that has been the plan all along."

"Thank you. I never imagined we would make it this far, but I hoped."

The camp spread out across the vast field, a line of tall pale grasses that swayed with the breeze. Wide olive trees dotted the area, brimming with fruit at the right time of year. There would be no time to taste and enjoy them. Steel was the only thing that would be tasted that day.

"Whatever happens today, let's face it together," Alexander told the others around him. "We have come this far. I will see you all in the heavens when we dine with the gods."

"Piss on death," Adrian replied.

"Well said," Timothy almost laughed.

"Back to the horses. I have a plan," Alexander told them.

They crawled through the tall grass, back below to a small hill where horses drank from a stream. Tightening girths and armor, they climbed on.

"Follow my lead. Pull your javelins out and do not hesitate to throw them. Ready for one last ride, girl?" Alexander asked Canyon. "Thank you for being here with me."

Javelins had been delivered on another cart for them, another gift from the king. Some didn't know how to use them, but any were better than none.

Please let these strike their targets. Hopefully they can all manage.

"Elbows high and use your momentum," Alexander told them.

Then heels hit against the horse as Alexander sped off, followed by the rest of his battered army. Up the short hill and toward the camp they stampeded. Enemy soldiers stood as javelins whirled through the air like angered hornets that stung with piercing blows. Alexander ploughed through the enemy soldiers. All around him they collapsed. Arrows whirled by, but he continued to release the couple of javelins he had from his quiver. Death whirled in the air from both directions.

Any moment is a good moment to die.

Spears struck out from the enemy, some striking metal with ear piercing scrapes. A quick glance behind him showed that everyone had fanned out like a V as they swept through the camp and released javelins that caused defenders to fall like shot geese as they ripped through shield and armor alike. Two men fell from their horses, blue cloaks tumbling into the dirt, but there was no way to stop now. Ahead of Alexander over the hill was the stunning city of Solaria that rested with two bodies of water to each side. Rivers carved out the city in various curves and directions. Water sparkled and the silver-like leaves of olive orchards became more frequent.

In and out of the city carts and people moved through the sunset gate. A soldier held a horn, but before he could blow it, Adrian cut off both hands and the horn cluttered to the ground.

"No horn today!" Adrian bellowed and dug into his horse. "Cunt!"

Down the hill horses streamed in browns, blacks, and grays. People jumped out of the way as there was no slowing down. A horn sounded on the wall. It was too late to keep the Order of Fate out. Fate seemed to be on their side as the gate was too large and too heavy to close before they reached it. Unprepared soldiers attempted to step in front of the gate but jumped out of the way as the horses barreled towards them. The citadel was on the eastern wall and that was where the stream of horses headed. Alexander would not hesitate at the gate and the stampede behind him would not be halted. Arrows clattered against stone from all directions. Doors slammed and windows shut as people ran into their homes to hide. Hooves hit against stone as the horses pressed on, frothing from their bits as riders pushed them to their limits.

The gate will be closed. Alexander looked around. *There is only one option.*

With a pull of the reins and a shift of his foot, Alexander turned the horse down a side street. Narrow streets of stone houses with eyes that stared at them from second and third floors, they continued.

Those have to be the stairs to the wall.

It was a gamble, but the entire journey had been so far. A wide-eyed soldier stood frozen as the horse surged toward him. Flattening against the horse, Alexander held on as the stone arching doorway was too close for comfort. The moment he entered, a sword swung at his leg. It glanced off his armor, causing pain to shoot up his leg. Using his leverage, Alexander split the man's head with ease. A second sword clattered as Chase killed the next soldier. Hooves stomped upon stairs as Canyon surged upward. Armor scraped stone as soldiers bounced against the wall of the grey staircase that winded its way up to the wall above.

"Crazy cunt!" Adrian shouted. "Let's go!"

Horses crowded the stairs and onto the wall, tossing soldiers from its height onto the ground below. A long stretch to the citadel, but that mattered not.

"This may be where we go our separate ways, Canyon." Alexander hugged her and gave her a pat. "You were a good horse. I don't think I will leave this place alive. Thank you for being faithful. I will never forget you, but there is no need for you to die with me."

Large eyes looked at him and nostrils flared, then she nudged him.

"I will take that as love. Be free. Lead the others away if you can."

The rest of the army had followed him onto the wall. Timothy, Chase, and Adrian all did the same. Any that didn't leave their horses below followed their four leaders. Many held their horses tight as they knew it was going to be the last hug they ever had. Some kissed their heads and others shed a few tears, then smacked their horse's rear. Each gave a heartfelt goodbye. Horses were a soldier's best friend more often than not. Then a stampede of horses ran along the wall.

"Order of Fate, let us deliver some justice! The gods are with us. Today, we become immortal."

"Sanctus Imperator!" The army returned with weapons raised above head.

As if bit in the ass, they moved forward. Many had been lost along the way, but today, there was only death to be had. Sword in hand, Alexander fingered the hilt, as he eyed the sore on the back of his hand. Then steps forward took him closer to the enemy that moved toward them six wide in their gold and red.

"Better pull out those shields," Alexander told them. "Work as one. Get in close. They are using spears."

Quick steps brought them closer to the enemy. On each side a sheer drop to death and in front of them was either death or victory.

"Tell your god that our three say hello," Alexander told the man in front of him.

Spearpoint scraped against the rectangular shield. Tips of silver gleamed as they streamed forward in unison, blocked by the shields. Swords from the second line of defense severed any that went over the shields, leaving the defenders to drop their spear and favor the sword. The grating of metal and shrieks of pain were all to be heard. Swords were quick to grow slick with blood in the dizzying fray of battle. Soldiers continued to pour on the wall, now on each side of them where they could.

"To the death!" Alexander shouted.

Shield walls held firm on each side of the Order, protecting those on the inside so that they could lash out with vicious strikes. Adrian pushed through to the eastern side of the wall. His rigorous battle prowess inspired others to fight harder. There was much to say about the man, but the fact that he had no fear was toward the top.

"Come on ya cunts! I will send you all to the makers!" A multitude of swings crashed upon them.

Each step became slippery as blood oozed along the top of the wall from limp bodies with whitened eyes. Adrian grunted as a sword penetrated his bicep, then struck a blow that partially severed the head from his attacker with a clean swipe. It was an odd feeling, the lightness of battle. Heavy, gut wrenching, but freeing. All around was death and chaos, but in that chaos, there was…serenity. Blood filled his mouth with iron has he held a firm grip on the sword. Perilous battle waged on along the wall overlooking the sea toward the citadel of Solaria. Pride swelled inside of Alexander as he made a move. With tremendous speed his sword swiped with the occasional strike of his target. Each movement had to be precise the further into battle you moved. Over the weeks his biceps and forearms had become poisoned steel, hard as any armor from the battles and training, even with the tenderness underneath. Timothy and Chase moved to his side as did the others. Forward motion took the defense by surprise as they stumbled and fell backward.

"Take the center!" Alexander shouted. "Force them over."

They cleared the way and soldiers filed in by pairs using their shields to press against the Higanians and push them from the wall. Feet scraped against stone as each side attempted to gain leverage. A test of might, a battle of determination. Below, bodies fell like rain, some onto cliffs below near the sea, and others to the city floor.

Sweat poured from Alexander, but fatigue would not overwhelm him. It could not defeat the adrenaline that flushed through him like a cooling storm. Every bit of energy he had would be used in this battle. There would be nothing left to give after. Steel slid against his forearm, enough to leave a gash. Spinning around, he severed the man's head.

Step, thrust, parry, counter. Timothy moved fluid even in the tight quarter of the battle on the wall. Sword slid off sword, as the latter in one swift motion, dealt death. Blue eyes reflected cold steel with each swing. An arrow struck him in the thigh as he hunched down for a moment. Then sword scraped against his chest plate and across his biceps.

"No!" Adrian kicked the attacker backward then his blade took place of where the man's eyes once were.

Powerful swings with grunts hammered against defenders as the sword raised and fell. Larger than them, Adrian was fierce, a bear among the wall. Timothy joined him. Speed and power combined, the two were the perfect storm. Battering the enemy with wicked gales as blades whirled like the wind and struck like stone. Six, eight, fifteen fell to the two. Then an arrow struck Timothy's throat and dropped him where he stood. To his knees he dropped, both hands clutching his neck, but he didn't look on in terror. Alexander saw his eyes, eyes that were proud. With a guttural growl, Adrian surged forward. Any in his way were set to die. Reaching the archer a few rows back, he gauged out his eyes.

"Blind to the underworld you go, filthy cunt!" Then he tossed him from the wall.

Three swords turned Adrian into a pin cushion as they plunged through armor. Grasping his sword once more, he fought them back with shouts. Each swing he lost power, but still they circled him like vultures. Twice more the swords entered him, blood dripping from his mouth onto thick black hair, turning it slick. The large man collapsed. Hands pressed to the ground, the man groaned, as he crawled to Timothy's dead body. Wide hands stretched out as he reached him, closing his eyelids.

"Brothers." Adrian smiled and laid his head against the other.

There was no time for Alexander to avenge them or to be able to filter all of the information through his mind. Around him both sides died and all he could focus on was taking as many with him as he could.

"One last time, brother."

"One last time." Chase nodded.

Then the two moved in with any left behind them. The citadel was at the back of the defenders. Now they were upon it. Alexander and the remaining fifty soldiers moved onto the Citadel, battering the defenders back. Bloodied bodies, tattered cloaks, and determined faces pressed forward. From two sides the Higanian's flooded the field of battle. Body weakening, heavy breaths, and an arm that felt like a limp leaf, Alexander still pressed on. *Feint*, then *lunge*—another one fell. *Disarm*, the sword clattered on stone, then *thrust*—another down. Repeated movements to keep the enemy at bay and push them back. *The last stand.*

A smile came over Alexander's face which caused the soldier

in front of him to freeze. It was impossible not to look around at the beautiful day with seagulls floating above in the sky. Death was all around, but still beauty found a way as the citadel was pressed by the hands of the Order of Fate. Few admiral blue cloaks still swayed in the battle, but they still swayed. Forever, they would sway in the memories of the Higanians, they would remember the blue cloaks and the snake for eternity. Those that ripped their greedy hands off with blades. Those that showed the mighty empire what it meant when death had no cost. Another blade drove down at him but was deflected as it slid and screeched.

Blood poured from his wounds and Chase's as well. Still, they fought, weakening with each blow, each moment life continued to drain from them. Chase's hand clung to his brother's shoulder.

"I love you, Alex."

"I love you too, Chase. I am sorry."

"Don't be. We go out fighting, together. You have always been my idol. It is an honor to die at your side. There is no better day than today to meet the gods. If I meet them, I am glad you will be next to me. Promise me we will walk through the gates together."

"Nowhere else I would rather be. I promise. On your left."

Alexander lazily lunged forward and managed to pierce the attackers throat. Then a sword plunged into his ribs. Warm steel moving up, further up, releasing the pain of life in one breath. His spirit surged from his body and back down as the sword pulled out and he collapsed. It was as if time slowed as Chase killed the man, tears staining his cheek, mixing with the blood of his or others. Two more fell to his brother who began to fight like a mad dog with nothing left to lose.

A horn? Was that a horn? It had to be, but from where?

A faint sound seemed like it stemmed from the wall.

Someone save Chase. I will wait at the gate but save him. I don't mind waiting.

Multiple times he attempted to move, but life drained out of him. Muscles turned to melted snow and breathing became difficult.

Chase. Entienne. Entienne.

For a moment he saw her face, the face that he desired to touch more than anything. It was as if light itself bathed him. Bones no longer ached. Skin no longer hurt. Chase fell in front of him, eyes staring up at him.

Chase. Brother.

Alex reached out his hand. Chase grabbed it as his fingers went limp, eyes instantly glazing over.

It is over. It is all over.

"He is here!" Soldiers shouted.

Entienne?

The face of his wife turned into some strange soldier he had never seen. Soldiers with Sienna banners and armor flooded the citadel.

The clash continued, but it no longer mattered. They did it, they freed the citadel. Death meant something after all.

"Rest in peace. All will know your name. That is a promise. You won this today." Captain Dannilon knelt near him, his voice sounding far away. "Your soldiers will receive honors and a proper burial. I will make sure of it."

No words. Alexander couldn't speak. All he could muster was a smile. Admiral blue draped him as the wind blew his cloak over his leg.

"Entienne."

They came from nowhere. Blue cloaks like a wave of the sea crashed into the Higanian warriors—crushing them like ants in a rainstorm. When we attempted to greet the heroes, they sped off, never to be found. – Letter to the king

10

Chapter 10

Please leave a review on Amazon and Goodreads. I appreciate you.

www.ingramcontent.com/pod-product-compliance
Lightning Source LLC
Chambersburg PA
CBHW031359060726
47590CB00007B/2851